W9-AUQ-239

# Stink

Megan McDonald        illustrated by

# K

## and the Incredible Super-Galactic Jawbreaker

Peter H. Reynolds

SCHOLASTIC INC.
New York Toronto London
Auckland Sydney Mexico City
New Delhi Hong Kong Buenos Aires

No part of this publication may be reproduced, stored in
a retrieval system, or transmitted in any form or by any
means, electronic, mechanical, photocopying, recording, or
otherwise, without written permission of the publisher. For
information regarding permission, write to Candlewick Press,
2067 Massachusetts Avenue, Cambridge, MA 02140.

ISBN-13: 978-0-439-02273-6
ISBN-10: 0-439-02273-8

Text copyright © 2006 by Megan McDonald.
Illustrations copyright © 2006 by Peter H. Reynolds.
All rights reserved. Published by Scholastic Inc.,
557 Broadway, New York, NY 10012, by arrangement with
Candlewick Press. SCHOLASTIC and associated logos are
trademarks and/or registered trademarks of Scholastic Inc.

12 11 10 9 8 7 6 5 4 3 2 1          7 8 9 10 11 12/0

Printed in the U.S.A.                    40

This edition first printing, January 2007
This book was typeset in Stone Informal.
The illustrations were created digitally.

for Joseph, Jodi, and Matthew
M. M.

To Gary Goldberger, my super-galactic
creative partner on the journey
P. H. R.

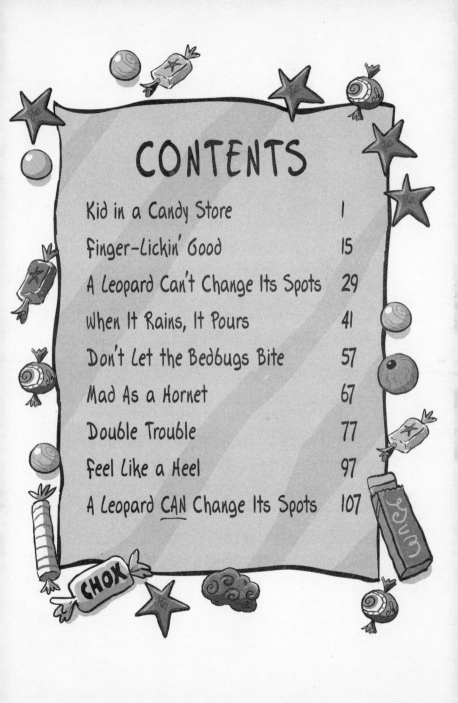

# CONTENTS

# Kid in a
# Candy
# Store

Gigantic!

Super-colossal!

Inter-galactic!

Stink stood smack in the middle of the Whistle Stop Candy Shop. Shelves all around him were chock-full of sourballs, penny candy (that cost ten cents), licorice shoelaces, gummy money, candy pebbles, spooky-eye gumballs, wax fangs, buttered-popcorn jellybeans, bottle caps, chocolate Scottie dogs, and mood lollipops.

Then he saw it. Right smack in the middle of it all.

Hello! Welcome to Planet Jawbreaker! Super-galactic jawbreakers! Stink reached to pick one up. It was an earth, a globe, a world unto itself. A speckled, sparkling planet. Bigger than a marble. Bigger than a Super Ball. Bigger than a golf ball. World's largest jawbreaker! Or at least the biggest Stink had ever seen in his whole entire seven years on the planet.

Stink's sister, Judy, ran up to him. "Look, Stink, they have bubblegum baloney and lollipops that play music

and real-and-true rain-forest gum and best of all . . . gummy brains! I can't decide WHAT you're getting me!"

"Your brains are gummy if you think I'm buying you stuff," Stink told his big sister. Sometimes big sisters were so double-triple-quadruple bossy.

"C'mon, Stink. Don't be a sourball. You have a big fat five-dollar gift certificate."

"I earned it! Dad took me to the college, and I was in a study for short people. I had to answer really hard questions."

"Stink, I can't help it if I'm not short!

4

Please, pretty please, with gummy brains on top? Just one candy cell phone? Purple candy corn? A diamond-ring lollipop? I know, I know! If you won't buy me candy, how about this How-to-Make-Your-Own-Gum kit?"

"No, no, no, no, and nope."

"C'mon, Stinker. Just one teeny-weeny piece of candy? How much can one piece of penny candy cost?"

"Ten cents. Some penny candy costs twenty-five cents."

"Huh? How can something that costs a penny cost a quarter?"

"Beats me," said Stink.

Stink's sister, Judy, was in a mood. She slumped down on the car-seat couch in the corner of the candy store. She pretended to watch the Oompa-Loompas dancing on the TV screen in front of her. Stink popped from one shelf to the next, filling his basket with suckers and sourballs, gumballs and gummy worms.

"Stink, I'm telling Dad you're acting like a kid in a candy store," said Judy.

"But I AM a kid in a candy store," said Stink. "Hey! You just said an idiom."

"I am NOT an idiot!" said Judy.

"Id-i-om. It's what you call a funny

saying. Mrs. D. taught us a bunch of them. Like if you're in a bad mood, I could say you got up on the wrong side of the bed."

"But I'm not in a bad mood, because you're going to get me some candy, right?"

"Wrong."

"Is *stinks on ice* an idiom? How about *rotten to the core*?" said moody Judy.

"Now you're acting like sour grapes," said Stink. "Get it? *Sour grapes* is another idiom."

"Stop saying *idiom!*" said Judy.

"Okay! Okay! If I get you candy,

what will you give me?" asked Stink. *"Let's strike a deal.* Get it?"

Judy rolled her eyes. "How about one Grouchy pencil and two president baseball cards for this box of rain-forest gum?"

"*Three* president baseball cards," said Stink. "And one of them has to be James Madison."

"Deal," said Judy. "Goody goody gumdrops! Thanks, Stink. Now, Richie Rich, let me see what you're getting yourself with all that money."

"I," said Stink, "am getting the World's Biggest Jawbreaker." He held it

up for Judy to see. "It changes colors and flavors as you go."

"Rare! It looks like an earth. Or a giant emu egg or something."

"Or something," said Stink.

"Stink, I don't think you want to eat

that. Says here on the box that it contains wax."

"Does not."

"Does too!" Judy pointed to the words on the box.

"So? I've eaten wax before."

"Have not."

"Have too."

"Stink, wax is like candles," said Judy. "Wax is like earwax. Are you going to eat EARwax, Stink?"

"Give it," said Stink, taking it back. "Stop saying *earwax*! I'm still eating it. It has fire in the middle."

"Like a fireball?"

"Like the earth's core!" said Stink.

"RARE!" said Judy. "Do you think it'll really break your jaw?"

"It better!" said Stink.

# It's Just Sour Grapes! by Stink Moody

AFTER A LONG, HARD LOOK AT BOTH BUNCHES OF GRAPES, JELLY MAN SAID...

I choose the purple grapes to become jelly!

YAY! YIPPEE! YAHOOO!

GRRRR! WHO WANTS TO BE MADE INTO STICKY OLD JELLY ANYWAY?!

You're just being a bunch of SOUR GRAPES, which makes SOUR Jelly. You'll make GREAT raisins, though.

You'll make some bran very happy.

Hmmph!

# Finger-Lickin' Good

**S**tink took one lick. Then another. Then another. The giant jawbreaker was way too big to fit into his mouth.

*Slurp.* He licked that jawbreaker all the way home.

*Sloop.* He licked it all the way up to his room.

*Slop.* He licked it while he fed Toady one-handed. He licked it while he played with his president baseball cards (including James Madison, thanks to Judy). He licked it while he did his

homework one-handed. He licked it the whole time he talked to Grandma Lou on the phone, telling her all about the Pajama Day they were going to have in Mrs. D.'s class.

He even licked it while he set the table for dinner. One-handed, of course.

Pretty soon his lips were green and his tongue was blue and his hands were as sticky as gum on a sneaker bottom.

"Hey," Judy asked at dinner. "Why is there a big fat sticky blue fingerprint on my plate?"

"Oops," said Stink, licking off his fingers. "Finger-lickin' good!"

"Stink's eating a jawbreaker for dinner!" said Judy, pointing.

"Stink, put that jawbreaker down and eat some real food," said Dad. "Here. Have some macaroni."

"This *is* real food," said Stink. "It contains vitamins A and C and calcium. No lie."

"And dextrose, sucrose, fructose, and other stuff that makes you comatose," said Judy.

"It's NOT going to make me comb my toes," said Stink.

"And don't forget wax," said Judy.

"Macaroni," said Mom. "You heard Dad. And green beans."

"But it didn't break my jaw yet," said Stink. "It didn't even stretch my mouth one bit."

"You already have a big mouth," said Judy.

"Hardee-har-har," said Stink. "Well, it didn't set my tongue on fire yet or make my cheeks feel like a chipmunk, either."

"It may not break your jaw," said Judy, "but all your teeth are going to fall out. For sure and absolute positive. Did you know Queen Elizabeth ate so many candies from her pockets that her teeth turned black? No lie!"

"At least I won't have to brush them every day!" said Stink.

* * *

Every day, Stink ate a little more and a little more of his jawbreaker. He ate it in bed first thing in the morning before he brushed his teeth. He ate it at recess in between playing H-O-R-S-E with his super-duper best friend, Webster. He ate it on the bus and all the way home from school.

He gave a lick to Mouse the cat. He gave a lick to Toady the toad. He even tried giving a lick to Jaws the Venus flytrap.

Stink's jawbreaker went from super-galactic to just plain galactic. From golf-ball size to Super-Ball size.

"Are you still eating that thing?" asked Judy. Stink stuck out his tongue.

"Well, you look like a skink," said Judy. She pointed to his blue tongue.

*Shloop!* went Stink.

Stink ate his not-super-galactic jawbreaker for one whole week. He ate it when it tasted like chalk. He ate it when it tasted like grapefruit. He ate it through the fiery core to the sweet, sugary center. He ate it down to a marble. A teeny-tiny pea.

Then, in one single bite, one not-jaw-breaking crunch, it was G-O-N-E, gone.

Stink was down in the dumps. He moped around the house for one whole day and a night. He stomped up the stairs. He stomped down. He drew comics. *Ka-POW!* He did not play with Toady once. He did not do his homework. He went outside and bounced Judy's basketball 117 times.

"Somebody got up on the WRONG side of the bed," said Judy. "If I didn't know better, I'd think you were in a MOOD."

"I can have moods too, you know." Stink kept counting. "One hundred

eighteen, one hundred nineteen . . ."

"Is it because your jawbreaker's all gone?" asked Judy.

"It's because that jawbreaker lied. They should call it World's Biggest UN-jawbreaker. I ate and ate that thing for one whole week, and it did not break my jaw. Not once. It didn't even make my mouth one teeny-weeny bit bigger.

See?" Stink clicked and clacked his teeth open and shut.

"Maybe that's a good thing," said Judy. "I mean, if it did break your jaw for real, wouldn't you be mad?"

"Yeah, but instead I'm madder." Stink had an idea. A brilliant what-to-do-when-you're-mad idea. Stink would write a letter. A real-and-true official snail-mail letter. A letter with a greeting and a body and a closing, just the way Mrs. D. taught them in their how-to-write-a-letter unit at school.

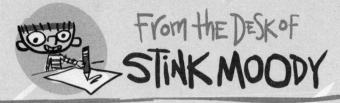
# From the Desk of
# STINK MOODY

## Dear Mr. or Mrs. Jawbreaker,

*(THIS IS CALLED A GREETING)*

My name is Stink Moody. I got $5.00 for being short and I spent it on a super-galactic jawbreaker (and some NOT-penny candy for my sister).

There is a big problem with your jawbreaker. It did NOT (I repeat NOT) break my jaw. For your information, all it did was get me in trouble at the dinner table and make me look like a skink. In my opinion, you should change the name jawbreaker to Super Not-Galactic Mouth Crayon.

Yours Truly, *(THIS IS CALLED A CLOSING)*
## Stink (THE SKINK) MOODY

**P.S.** It did not even break the jaw of Jaws, my sister's Venus flytrap. *(THIS IS CALLED A POSTSCRIPT)*

# A Leopard Can't Change Its Spots

Exactly eleven days later, a package arrived for Stink. A box that thumped and clunked when he shook it. A box that rattled and crunched when he opened it. A big box full of . . . jawbreakers!

Stink read the letter. "Dear Mr. Stink Moody, blah blah. While we are not in the business of breaking jaws . . . blah blah blah . . . sorry that our jawbreaker did not meet your satisfaction . . . more blah . . . please accept an assortment of fun, exciting and brand-new jaw-breakers you might like . . ."

"Holy jawbreaker heaven!" There were mega jawbreakers, mini jawbreakers, monster jawbreakers, black, rainbow, and psychedelic jawbreakers, asteroids and alien heads, glow-in-the-darks and gobstoppers, even jawbreaker lollipops on a stick with a bubblegum center.

"Leaping lollipops!" squealed Judy. "Where'd you get all these? There's more jawbreakers here than in Willy Wonka's house." She tossed a handful up in the air.

"Ten whole pounds!" said Stink. "It says so right here. Wait till I tell Webster!"

"That's 21,280 jawbreakers!" Judy pointed to the number on the box.

"What am I gonna do with twenty thousand million jawbreakers?"

"Get twenty thousand million cavities, of course," said Judy. "C'mon, let's divide them up. We can each set up our own jawbreaker store and trade them with each other. Or we could start our own jawbreaker museum."

"What do you mean WE?" asked Stink.

"You and me," Judy said. "Two heads are better than one. I mean two *jawbreaker eaters* are better than one."

"No way are you getting half!" said Stink. "They're mine-all-mine, and I get to decide."

"Stink, you never share!"

"You know what they say . . . You can't teach an old dog new tricks! A leopard can't change its spots! Besides, I'm the one who wrote the letter."

"What letter?"

"I wrote a letter to the jawbreaker company about how my super-galactic jawbreaker did not break my jaw."

"No fair!" said Judy. "I wrote a letter once that you, my little brother, wrecked my Hedda-Get-Betta doll, and all I got from the doll company was a get-well card."

Stink cracked up.

"Are you sure you didn't win a contest for being short or something?" Judy asked.

"Honest! All I did was write one puny little letter."

Suddenly, Stink had an idea. Not a puny little idea. A great big super-galactic idea.

If Stink could write one letter, he could write two . . . three . . . four! It would be just like homework. Mrs. D. said practice makes perfect. If he wrote more letters, he could get more free stuff. And if he got more free stuff, he'd be like a bazillionaire!

Stink took out his best writing-a-real-letter paper. At the top it said, FROM THE DESK OF STINK MOODY.

Stink started to write. He wrote and wrote and wrote. He used his best-ever A+ penmanship. He wrote until his hand felt like it was falling off. Three whole letters! Mrs. D. would give him a triple Golden Pen rubber stamp for extra, extra, extra credit.

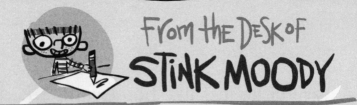

FROM THE DESK OF
STINK MOODY

Dear Kandy Kompany,

Did you know your Kool Katz chocolate bar is spelled wrong? Everybody, even the World's Worst Speller, my sister, Judy, knows CATS is spelled C-A-T-S. Not K-A-T-Z. I think the name of your candy company is spelled wrong, too. Maybe you never heard of the letter C? (Comes after A and B!) In your ads, you say "Gimme a break!" I say, "Give ME a break."

Signed,

Stink

P.S. Your chocolate is messed up, too. It's WHITE!

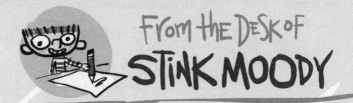

Dear Robo Toys,

I got a microbot with my lunch at House of Burgers. At first, it was way cool. It has eyes that light up and ears that go up and down, and it is called Burp, but I guess you know that. You say on your package that your mini robots will listen and do what I tell them. You say they will amaze me. I told Burp to mess up my sister's room. He did not mess up one thing! All he did was burp at the dinner table. It amazed me that I didn't get in trouble.

I even read all the directions. I mean ALL. Even the french ones.

Sincerely Un-amazed,

Stink

P.S. It says an astronaut thought up my toy. Maybe you should send the Amazingly Boring Burp back to outer space.

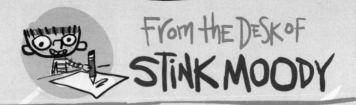
FROM THE DESK OF
STINK MOODY

Dear City Parks,

I went to a park near my house called Monkey Island. First of all, can I just tell you it is not an island. Second of all, there are NO monkeys. I looked up in the trees, in the jungle gym, behind rocks. I even looked in the trash cans. P.U.! I did not see one single monkey the whole entire time. Not even a monkey bar! My sister knows big dictionary words, and she said this is called false advertising. I could really use some tickets to the zoo to see some real monkeys. And lemurs.

In closing,

Stink

# When It Rains, It Pours

Once he started, Stink could not stop writing letters. He wrote a letter to Webster (the friend, not the dictionary). He wrote a letter to his other best friend, Elizabeth, who liked to be called Sophie of the Elves. He even wrote a letter to his teacher, telling her how great he was at writing letters.

At school, when Mrs. Dempster put a sample letter on the board, full of mistakes, Stink found every single goof, including *Deer Sirs* and *Yours Untruly*.

"Stink, you really put your thinking cap on today!" said Mrs. D. "Now, who can tell me what the best part of writing a letter is?" she asked.

"When you're done?" asked Webster.

"Cool stamps?" asked Sophie of the Elves.

"When somebody writes back!" said Mrs. D.

"Especially when they write back

with like about a million jawbreakers,"
said Stink.

"Speaking of a million, it's time for
math," said Mrs. D.

✳ ✳ ✳

Waiting sure was bor-ing. UN-amazing.
Stink came home from school and
checked the mailbox first thing every
day. He did not get one puny letter. Not
even a postcard! Not from the candy
company that couldn't spell *cat*. Not
from the toy company with the
microbot that wouldn't listen. Not from
the city park with no monkeys.
Nothing. Nada. Zip. Zero.

"Maybe my letters got lost," said Stink.

"Maybe they know you're just trying to get free stuff," said Judy.

"Am not."

"Are too."

"Maybe I forgot to put stamps on them," said Stink.

"Maybe your letters were abducted by alien microbots," said Judy.

"Hardee-har-har. So funny I forgot to laugh."

* * *

Then one day it happened, all at once.

"When it rains, it pours," Mom said.

Stink did not see any rain, but he did see a package. From the toy company. He tore open the box. Microbots! Monsters and spotted dogs and striped cats. Blue lions and pink mice and even a koala!

Stink read the card. "It says since my microbot didn't work, try these!"

"No fair!" said Judy. "You have all the luck."

"Knock on wood," said Stink. Just then there was a knock on the (wood!) door. Judy ran to open it.

"Package," said the delivery guy. "For a Mr. Stink Moody."

"Nobody lives here with that name," said Judy.

"Do too!" said Stink. He dropped his bots and ran to the door.

"Sign here," said the guy.

"He can't even write cursive!" said Judy.

"Can too!" said Stink, printing his name with curlicues to look like cursive.

Stink shook the box. "I wonder what it is. . . ."

"I wonder," said Judy. "Could it be about one million Kool Katz bars?"

"It says here they spelled *Katz* with a *K* on purpose because they thought it would look *kool*. But they're sending me free stuff for my trouble."

Judy tried to open the box. "Hey, let me!" said Stink. His jaw dropped open.

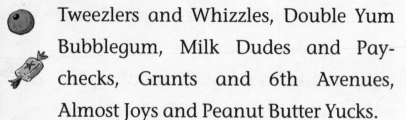

Tweezlers and Whizzles, Double Yum Bubblegum, Milk Dudes and Pay-checks, Grunts and 6th Avenues, Almost Joys and Peanut Butter Yucks.

"RARE!" said Judy. "I've never seen so many candy bars."

"And don't forget the jar of chocolate-chip peanut butter, the mint green chocolate crossword puzzle, and the Kool Katz baseball cap!"

"Triple rare!" said Judy.

"And it's F-R-E-E, free." said Stink. "Free as a bird! And all mine!"

Judy was mint green with envy. She wished she'd gotten two tons of special-

delivery, sign-in-cursive free candy and stuff. "Stink, you can't just keep all this stuff. It's like stealing or something."

"Or something," said Stink. "No way am I giving it back. I didn't take it."

Just then the phone rang. "Stink, it's for you," said Mom. "They asked for Mr. Moody, and they don't mean Dad."

Mom passed the phone to Stink and went back into her office.

"Yes, I'm him. . . . Uh-huh. . . . Really? No lie? . . . How many do I want? . . . I can have twenty-five? . . . With monkeys? Okay. . . . Yes, I think I would be satisfied."

"What?" asked Judy.

"It was the City Parks Department. I get a whole bunch of FREE monkey pencils and one free pass to the zoo! To go see monkeys! And lemurs!"

"I'm telling," said Judy. "Mo-om!"

"Shh!" said Stink.

Mom came back into the front room. "It's no fair," Judy told her. "Stink gets tons of free stuff and he won't give me ANY and I wrote a letter one time and all I got was a big fat nothing."

"Stink?" asked Mom. "What's this all about?"

"Nothing!" said Stink.

"It doesn't look like nothing."

"Okay, okay. Mrs. D. taught us how to write letters and I was just practicing, you know, like homework . . ."

"Ha!" said Judy.

"And maybe I sent some letters to some people. . . ."

"Companies!" said Judy. "Begging for free stuff!"

"No way!" said Stink. "I just told them some stuff that was wrong with things, and they sent me all this! And it's free, and no way is it stealing!" said Stink.

"Stink," said Mom, "no more letters.

Later on we'll talk to Dad about what to do with all this stuff."

"Do we have to send it back?" asked Stink.

"We'll see," said Mom.

"Ha!" Judy whispered. "That means YES!"

# Don't Let the Bedbugs Bite

After that, the mail got way boring. No exciting letters, no mysterious packages. Stink got a postcard about wearing a seat belt, a new issue of *Short Stuff* magazine, and some envelope addressed in super-messy writing. He didn't bother opening it. Bor-ing!

Then, after dinner, as if Mom had read his mind, she told Stink out of the blue, "I almost forgot. A box came for you. It's on the table."

"Not *another* one," said Judy, hitting her forehead. "No fair. Stink, you're not supposed to write any more letters."

"I didn't!" said Stink. "I swear!"

"Don't worry. It's from someone you know and love this time."

"Jawbreaker Heaven? Gobstoppers? I know and love them."

"No. Grandma Lou. She heard about Pajama Day."

"Pajama Day?" asked Judy.

"It's only in Mrs. D.'s class," said Stink.

"We get to bring stuffed animals and a sleeping bag and wear pajamas and stuff. Then we read books all day and we don't have math and she brings her dog."

"What does her dog have to do with Pajama Day?" asked Judy.

"I'm just saying," said Stink.

"How come Stink gets a present and not me?" asked Judy.

"It's not a present," said Stink. "It's for Pajama Day. That's like homework."

"Just my luck," said Judy. "I have math and spelling, and Stink gets pajama homework." She peered over Stink's shoulder as he opened the box.

"Stop crowding," said Stink. "I need my personal space."

Judy reached into the box and snatched something. "Look! I got a Bonjour Bunny shirt!"

"How come you get that?" asked Stink.

"For Un-pajama Day!" said Judy.

Stink pulled out a pair of striped PJs with bacon and eggs all over them. "No way am I wearing these for Pajama Day," said Stink.

"Why not?" asked Mom.

"Hello! Kindergarten!" said Stink.

"Well, I think they're cute as a bug's ear," said Mom.

Mouse raced over and licked the pajama eggs.

"Mouse likes them!" said Judy. "Look, Stink. The sunny-side-up eggs have glow-in-the-dark middles! You love stuff that glows."

"Wait. Let me see," said Stink.

"Just try them on, honey," said Mom.

Stink pulled off his shirt and put on the pajama top. He stretched his arms out and turned back and forth, showing off.

"Stink, you look like a walking menu. No, a night-light! No, an electric eel!" said Judy. "How will you ever get to sleep?"

"It's better than the I ♥ TRUCKS ones I got last year," said Stink. "Besides, the glow-in-the-dark part is kool-with-a-*k*!" All of a sudden, Stink started to squirm. He scratched his arm. He scratched his neck. He pulled at the tag in back.

"What's wrong?" asked Judy. "Your new PJs have cooties?"

"These pajamas itch," said Stink.

"Here, I'll cut off the tags and soften them up in the washer for tomorrow,"

said Mom. "You get ready for bed now, Stink. You too, Judy."

"Good night! Don't let the bedbugs bite!" Dad called from the kitchen.

"But can't I stay up until my new PJs are done?" asked Stink.

"You mean until your homework's done?" Judy laughed. "Stink loves homework so much he wants to wear it!"

# CUTE AS A BUG'S EAR

IDIOM COMICS presents

by Stink Moody

**COOL!** A MAGNIFYING GLASS!

**OH!** LOOK AT THE TEENY TINY BUGS!

STINK SAW A BUG UP CLOSE.

**WOW!** I CAN EVEN SEE YOUR CUTE LITTLE EARS!

THANKS, STINK. MOST PEOPLE THINK I'M **UGLY.**

YOU'RE NOT **UGLY,** JUST **BUGLY!**

# Mad As a Hornet

The next morning, Stink woke up on the sunny-side-up side of bed. He did not even count his jawbreakers or play with his microbots. Today was the day he got to wear glow-in-the-dark pajamas to school! Double kool-with-a-*k*!

He ran downstairs. He looked under Mouse. He looked in the laundry-pile jumble on the couch. He looked on top of the washing machine. Where were his glow-in-the-dark pajamas?

That's when he saw it.

A great big ball of lint. Not just any old mousy gray lint. A super-galactic, neon-bright, glow-in-the-dark ball of not-gray lint.

UH-OH! If this was what he thought it was, Stink was going to be mad as a hornet! He ran to find Mom.

"Stink, honey," she told him, "I'm sorry to tell you that there was a problem with the new pajamas."

Problem pajamas? Pajamas should not have problems. Math tests should have problems. Brainteasers should have problems. Inventors should have problems.

"This?" Stink held out the super-galactic planet-size lint ball.

"I'm afraid so," said Mom. "One wash and all the glow stuff rubbed off."

Just then, Judy rushed into the room. "Look at me! My brand-new Bonjour Bunny shirt. It turned alien green. I look like a lime lollipop!"

"You mean my glow-in-the-dark stuff rubbed off on her?"

"Huh?" asked Judy.

Mom held up the pajamas. The bacon was just black wavy lines. And the sunny-side-up eggs were sunny-side-down brown mud pies.

"No way can I wear those!" said Stink.

"Think of it as scrambled eggs, Stink," said Judy.

"I could try sending them back to Grandma Lou," said Mom. "Maybe she can take them back. But you won't have any new pajamas to wear today. Your choice."

Pajama Day was going to be a big fat flop. Instead of way-cool glow-in-the-dark PJs, all Stink had to wear was a lousy lint ball.

"Send them back," said Stink. "Those bacon and eggs are toast."

Mom still made him write a thank-you letter to Grandma Lou, to send back with the pajamas.

Dear Grandma Lou,

Thank you but no thank you for the pajamas. At first I thought they were for babies, and Judy said I looked like a walking menu. Then I saw they glow in the dark and I changed my mind, but all the glow stuff rubbed off and now I look like scrambled eggs. So I M sending them back 2 U.

I hope they didn't cost an arm and a leg and you can take them back. If not, maybe give them to the Museum of Not-Glow-in-the-Dark Pajamas.

Maybe next time, you could send me something besides homework pajamas? (Not jawbreakers, though.)

Love, Stink

While Stink was writing his letter, Judy took the pajamas upstairs. She was up there all during breakfast. When she came back down, she announced, "Stink, I solved your pajama problem!"

"Huh?" asked Stink.

Judy dragged Stink by the arm into the coat closet and shut the door. Hey! Something glowed! Like a night-light! Like a thousand and one fireflies!

"My pajamas!" said Stink. "What did you . . . ? How did you . . . ?"

"I painted them with glow-in-the-dark paint!" said Judy. "So you don't have to send them back. The eggs are jellyfish now, and the bacon strips are electric eels!"

"Jumping jawbreakers!" said Stink. "Thanks!" He hugged his sister. "This is the way-coolest ever! Now I won't be the only kid in the whole second grade without cool pajamas. And I'll be the only one who glows!"

"Does this mean I can have a free candy bar now?" asked Judy.

"We'll see," said Stink.

# That Costs an Arm and a Leg by Stink Moody

THE NEW ART STORE IS OPEN!

THE DOT SPOT ARTS & CRAFTS

STINK FOUND JUST WHAT HE WANTED.

WOW!

THE ROBO·PEN 3000! IT REMEMBERS WHAT YOU DRAW AND CAN DRAW ALL BY ITSELF!

COOL DOODLE!

ROBO·PEN 3000

I SAY NICE THINGS ABOUT YOUR ART!

STINK LOOKED AT THE PRICE....

I'VE ONLY GOT TWENTY DOLLARS, BUT I'LL GIVE MY RIGHT ARM TOO!

THROW IN YOUR LEFT LEG AND YOU'VE GOT A DEAL.

MAN, THAT'S ONE PRICEY PEN!!

# Double Trouble

When Stink got to class 2D, his teacher was wearing a fuzzy THINK PINK bathrobe! She also had bunny slippers and a pillow and a real-live dog with bad breath named Pickles.

Stink forgot all about sunny-side-down eggs. He forgot about giant lint balls. What in the world could be better than wearing not-itchy, glow-in-the-dark pajamas to school and reading all day!

Stink plopped his sleeping bag next to his super-best-friend, Webster. "Are those your pajamas?" he asked.

"They're not my soccer uniform," said Webster. "But how would you know? I got them for my birthday."

Webster sure was being a grump. Stink did not know why. He hunkered down inside his sleeping bag and stuck his nose in a pop-up book of animal skeletons. He propped his head up on Fang, his six-foot-long stuffed-animal snake. He popped a FREE fireball in his mouth.

"Want one?" he asked Webster.

"You're not allowed to eat candy in school," said Webster. He turned the other way and stuck his nose in a book.

"Stink? Webster? Did you hear?" asked Sophie of the Elves. "We're having a Pajama Parade. We get to walk through all the halls. And we get to go to a special assembly in the library, where Mrs. Mack will tell stories from around the world. And she wears hats and plays drums. And I get to sit by you guys."

"Who cares?" said Webster.

"What's wrong with him?" Stink asked Sophie. Sophie just shrugged.

WOW! PAJAMA PARADE! ASSEMBLY! Assemblies in the library were the best! Stink could not wait to hear stories from around the world (with hats and drums).

Mrs. D.'s second-grade class paraded past the office and even down the fifth-grade hall. In the library, Stink sat beside Sophie of the Elves. Webster was right behind Stink. Mrs. D. pointed for Webster to sit down in the space right next to Stink.

"I'm not sitting by him," said Webster.

"Let's not make a mountain out of a molehill," said Mrs. D.

Webster sat down.

Mrs. Mack, the librarian, held up two fingers. "Let's show what good listeners we are at the Virginia Dare School," said Mrs. Mack.

"And remember," said Mrs. D., "let's keep our hands to ourselves."

Stink couldn't stand being ignored. Especially by his best friend. As soon as Mrs. Mack started to tell a story, Stink tapped Webster on the shoulder when he wasn't looking, just for fun.

"Hey!" said Webster. Stink pretended to be listening to the story. Webster tapped Stink on the shoulder, then pretended his hands were in his lap. Stink tapped him back. Webster tapped him back harder. "Ow!" said Stink.

"Stink!" whispered Mrs. D. She pointed

to Stink and Webster to settle down and keep quiet.

"You guys are in trouble!" whispered Sophie of the Elves.

"Now," said Mrs. Mack, "we're going to turn down the lights and travel to deepest Africa. I hope you like scary stories!"

The lights went out. Stink glowed like a night-light! Mrs. D. would sure see him now if he tapped Webster again. Stink pulled both of his arms all the way inside his pajama shirt, just to be safe. He did not want his tapping fingers to get him into any more trouble.

Drumbeats filled the air. Mrs. Mack made her voice low and whispery. The folktale was all about The Bad One, this spooky voice coming from inside a cave. The voice sounded so big and bad he was scaring the pants off all the other animals in the rain forest. At the end, The Bad One turned out to be nothing but a centipede. Phew! A South African red-legged centipede!

Stink knew all about centipedes. "Once, in the Toad Pee Club with my sister," he told Webster, "we tried to set a record for the longest human centipede."

"So?" said Webster.

Stink forgot all about paying attention. Something was wrong with Webster. He tried to make up a centipede joke to tell Webster.

"What goes ninety-nine clunk?" Stink asked Webster. "Or thirty-three clunk? Or sixty-seven clunk?" Webster ignored him. "A centipede with a broken leg!" Stink cracked up. He flashed his fireball-red tongue at Webster. Webster did not even crack a smile.

Mrs. Mack was asking, "How many legs does a centipede have?" Stink knew the answer. He went to raise his hand, but his arms were still inside his pajama shirt.

"One hundred!" said a first grader in the front row.

Stink knew one hundred was not the whole answer. He just had to raise his hand. He tried to raise an elbow from inside his shirt.

Something was wrong. Very wrong. Something had happened to Stink's pajama top. It shrink-shrank-shrunk! Stink wiggled and wriggled and tried to worm his way out of the shirt. Help!

Where were the armholes? It was still dark. He couldn't see a thing. His shirt was all twisted. His arms were all caught. His elbows poked inside his shirt like a punching bag, but he couldn't find his way out.

Help! Stink was stuck inside his pajama top!

"The name *centipede* means 'one hundred feet.' That's why we think all centipedes have a hundred legs," said Mrs. Mack.

Stink was still wrestling with his pajamas. The top went up over his head. Stink lost his head! He wrestled some more. Finally! He poked his arm out!

"Ow!" he heard Webster cry. "Hey, you sucker-punched me!" He shoved Stink into Sophie of the Elves.

"Hey!" said Stink. "I was only—"

"Boys!" said Mrs. D. "Come with me."

First the shirt. Then hitting Webster. Double trouble!

All the lights were on now. The room was suddenly somebody-got-in-trouble quiet. Webster had his head down and looked like he was going to cry. Everybody stared at the boys as they followed Mrs. Dempster out into the hallway.

"Okay, you two. What's this fighting all about? I thought you were the best of friends."

"Stink started it," said Webster. "I was

just sitting there, and he punched me for no reason."

"I didn't mean to hit him! Honest!" said Stink. "It's all my pajamas' fault. I got stuck inside my shirt! Cross my heart. No lie. I was just trying to raise my hand to say that most centipedes have fifteen pairs of legs. But some have up to 177 pairs, and if a leg gets cut off, it grows back, and some centipedes even glow in the dark."

"So it was an accident?" asked Mrs. Dempster.

"Yes!" said Stink.

"Can you say you're sorry, Stink?"

"Sorry, Webster," said Stink. "I didn't mean to hit you."

"Webster?" said Mrs. Dempster. "Are you okay now? Do you need to go see the nurse?"

"Whatever," said Webster.

"Boy," Stink said. "I never knew pajamas could get a person into so much trouble!" But Webster was already walking down the hall toward the nurse's office. His back was mad. Even his hair was mad.

IDIOM COMICS presents **Making a Mountain Out of a Molehill** by Stink Moody

HEY, MR. MOLE!! DAD'S GONNA BE MAD! YOU MADE OUR LAWN LOOK LIKE THE SURFACE OF THE **MOON**!

It's NO BIG DEAL—JUST A FEW BUMPS.

THE NEXT DAY...

I'LL show Stink what a **BIG** deal is....

YIKES!

And I thought **I** was making a mountain out of a molehill!

MOUNT MOLE

WANT TO GO MOUNTAIN CLIMBING WITH ME?

# Feel Like a Heel

Stink felt lousy. Worse than a NOT-one-hundred-legged centipede. He dragged himself home from school, down the street, up the sidewalk, and in the front door.

Dad was home early. "How was Pajama Day?" he asked Stink.

"Terrible," said Stink. "I had one of those terrible, horrible, no good, very bad, just-like-that-kids'-book yuck days."

"What's wrong?" asked Mom, coming into the room.

"Stink hit his friend Webster today!" said Judy. "At the library assembly. It was all over school. He got in way-big trouble and the teacher took him out and yelled at him up and down and the whole school saw and—"

"That's enough, Judy," said Dad.

"It wasn't my fault," said Stink. "It was my pajamas' fault!" Stink told Mom and Dad what happened. "I'm going to write a letter to the pajama people and tell them their pajamas got me in big trouble *and* made me lose my best friend," said Stink.

"No more letters!" said Judy.

"No more letters," said Mom.

"Well, maybe one more," said Dad. "How about a letter of apology to your friend Webster?"

Stink went upstairs. He hid the troublemaker PJs in the way-back of his bottom dresser drawer, where the pinchy underwear, socks with holes, and the too-baby I ♥ TRUCKS pajamas from last year were.

Then Stink worked on the letter as if it was homework.

Dear Webster,

I am really really really really really really really really sorry I punched you when I was just trying to tell about centipedes. Don't be mad at me anymore. Please please please with jawbreakers on top.

Sincerely,

Super-Sorry Stink

Stink searched around his desk for an envelope. He would put the letter on Webster's desk tomorrow. Hello! What was this? Under a pile of jawbreakers, Stink found an envelope. Not an empty envelope. A messy-handwriting envelope addressed to Stink Moody. As in him!

All of a sudden Stink remembered getting the messy-writing letter. But he'd been too busy counting his jawbreakers to even open it! He ripped it open now.

YOU ARE INVITED said the card. It was spelled out in balloons held by gorillas. The card was from Webster. It was for his birthday party. And his birthday party was Saturday. LAST Saturday.

Stink had missed Webster's birthday!

Now he knew why Webster was such a grump. Stink felt like a heel. No, he felt like 177 pairs of heels. Worse than a broken-legged centipede. Stink felt like a stinkbug.

He had to think of some way to make it up to Webster. They just had to be friends again. Had to!

Stink thought and thought. He petted Mouse. He petted Toady. He scratched his head a lot. Scratching your head was supposed to help you think, right? All it did was make him look like he had fleas.

At last, Stink got an idea. He went downstairs to get Dad in on his idea. Then he finished the letter to Webster.

P.S. I missed your party because I never got the invitation. I mean I got it but it was hiding under a LOT of jawbreakers. I guess I was so into my jawbreakers, I forgot everything else. You will get a special birthday surprise. Better than a letter. All I can say is LOOK OUT!

Hint: It starts with the letters C.G. (but you'll never ever guess!).

# IDIOM COMICS presents I Feel Like a Heel

by Stink Moody

STINK DID NOT SEE MOUSE SLEEPING....

MEEOOOWCH!

HEY, YOU HURT ME, MR. BIGFOOT!

I'M SORRY. I FEEL LIKE A REAL HEEL!

YOU LOOK like one too!

HEY!

YOU SMELL like one too!

# A Leopard

# CAN Change

# Its Spots

Stink got to school early and slipped the letter inside Webster's desk. He watched Webster read it. Webster looked up. He looked over at Stink. "You mean you didn't miss my birthday on purpose?"

"No way," said Stink. "Just like I didn't sucker-punch you on purpose. You gotta believe me."

Webster grinned from ear to ear.

"Friends?" asked Stink.

"Friends," said Webster. "So what's

the big surprise, huh? What's C.G.? C'mon! Tell me! I can't wait!"

"My lips are sealed," said Stink, zippering his lips.

"Does it stand for *Card Game*?" asked Webster.

"*Cinderella's Glass slipper?*" asked Sophie of the Elves.

"*Cucumbers and Grapes?*" asked Webster. "*Crazy Glue?*"

"No, no, and nope," said Stink. "You just have to wait. My dad's bringing it. But Mrs. D. said not until the end of the day."

Waiting was harder than writing letters. Harder than punctuation. Harder than spelling *sincerely.*

At the end of the day, Mrs. D. read eleven pages from Sophie of the Elves' favorite chapter book about a brave mouse and an evil rat.

Finally! At last! An announcement over the PA system.

"Special Delivery for Class 2D! Stink Moody to the front office!"

"Wow! Cool! Hey! What? Huh?" everybody buzzed.

Stink walked-not-ran down to the office and came back to class with Dad, a rainbow-bright rooster piñata, and 21,280 jawbreakers. Not to mention all sorts of candy bars, microbots, and monkey pencils.

"Candy-Gram!" Stink announced. "I repeat. Candy-Gram for Webster Gomez."

Webster was already at the door. He had never ever seen so much candy in his whole entire life. "For me? WOWEE!"

"To celebrate your birthday," said Stink. "With the whole class!"

"Piñata party!" everybody was saying.

"A Candy-Gram!" said Sophie of the Elves. "*C.G.* is for *Candy-Gram!*"

"I never got a Candy-Gram before. It's like a telegram, only better."

"Where'd you get all the candy and stuff?" asked Sophie.

"I got it FREE. Sort of by mistake on purpose."

Dad and Mrs. D. filled the piñata with

candy and goodies. Dad got to stand on the teacher's desk! He hung the piñata from the ceiling.

"Who wants to go first?" asked Dad, holding out the blindfold.

"Webster!" called Stink.

Dad put the blindfold on Webster and handed him the stick. "Stand back, everybody," Dad called.

"On the count of three!" said Mrs. D.

Webster swung the stick. It sliced the air, this way and that. *Whoosh! Swoosh!*

"Go, Webster, go!" everybody yelled. "Over this way. You're getting warm!"

*Bam!* Webster finally hit the piñata! Nothing. Class 2D was super-quiet.

"Let's try again—in French," said Mrs. D. "*Un, deux, trois . . .*" *Bam!* Webster hit the piñata again! Still nothing.

"That rooster doesn't want to crow," said Dad.

"I'll help!" called Stink. "Let's swing the stick together."

"Three's a charm," said Mrs. D. "Give it your best try. In Spanish, everybody! *Uno, dos, tres . . .*"

*Ka-POW!* Webster and Stink hit the piñata again. *Bam! Bam! Bam! Crack!* They cracked open the piñata.

*Cock-a-doodle-doo!* The rooster let out a loud sound, for real! Everybody screamed. A flood of candy rained down. Jawbreakers and Tweezlers, Milk Dudes and Peanut Butter Yucks. The kids raced to the front. They grabbed candy from all over the floor, under desks, behind the bookcase, even in the trash can.

"It's raining cats and dogs!" said Stink. "Kool Katz and Scottie dogs!"

"We really hit the jackpot!" said Webster.

"That was more fun than a barrel of monkeys!" said Sophie of the Elves.

"Marvelous! I can see we've really learned our idioms," said Mrs. D. "Now let's divide up all the treats fair and square. Share and share alike!"

Stink stared at his own sweet pile of treats and treasures on his desk. It was a lot smaller than 21,280 jawbreakers. But when he saw Webster's face, and a whole classfull of grins, he felt good inside. UN-rotten to the core, like the sweet, gooey bubblegum center of a jawbreaker.

"I'm proud of you, Stink," said Dad. "I think you proved a leopard CAN change its spots."

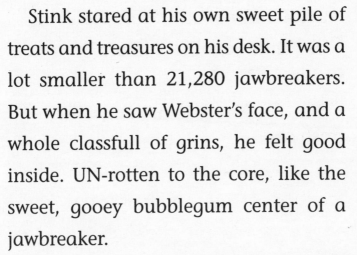

"I like the way you and your dad worked together," said Mrs. D., smiling. "Two heads *are* better than one."

"And friends are better than all the free stuff in the world," said Stink.

"Is that another idiom?" asked Webster.

"No, it's a Stink-iom!" said Stink.

# LIST OF IDIOMS
## (in order of appearance)

- kid in a candy store
- get up on the wrong side of the bed
- rotten to the core
- sour grapes
- strike a deal

- finger-lickin' good
- down in the dumps

- A leopard can't change its spots.
- Two heads are better than one.
- You can't teach an old dog new tricks.
- Practice makes perfect.

- When it rains, it pours.
- Put your thinking cap on.
- Knock on wood.
- jaw dropped open
- free as a bird
- green with envy

- Don't let the bedbugs bite.
- out of the blue
- just my luck
- cute as a bug's ear

- mad as a hornet
- cost an arm and a leg

- double trouble
- make a mountain out of a molehill
- lost his head
- cross my heart

- feel like a heel

- grin from ear to ear
- My lips are sealed.
- You're getting warm.
- Three's a charm.
- It's raining cats and dogs.
- hit the jackpot
- more fun than a barrel of monkeys
- fair and square
- Share and share alike.